Bleeping Beauty

For Cara Fachau,
with Seriously Silly wishes,

Visit   ə at

ORCHARD BOOKS
338 Euston Road
London NW3 3BH
Orchard Books Australia
Level 17-207 Kent Street, Sydney, NSW 2000, Australia

First published by Orchard Books in 2008
First paperback publication in 2009

Text © Laurence Anholt 2008
Illustrations © Arthur Robins 2008

The rights of Laurence Anholt to be identified as the author
and of Arthur Robins to be identified as the illustrator
of this work have been asserted by them in accordance
with the Copyright, Designs and Patents Act, 1988.

A CIP catalogue record for this book is available from the British Library.

ISBN 978 1 84616 073 8 (hardback)
ISBN 978 1 84616 311 1 (paperback)

1 2 3 4 5 6 7 8 9 10 (hardback)
1 2 3 4 5 6 7 8 9 10 (paperback)

Printed in China

Orchard Books is a division of Hachette Children's Books,
an Hachette Livre UK company.
www.hachettelivre.co.uk

seriously SILLY colour

Bleeping Beauty

ORCHARD BOOKS

Once upon a throne
sat a brand new baby Princess.
The King and Queen were so
happy; they had a big party and
invited the ten Good Fairies.

But they did NOT invite
the Hairy Scary Fairy.

All the Good Fairies made
a wish for the Princess ...

Wishy washy,
my name's Grace
She will have
a pretty face

Wishy washy,
my name's Claire
She will have
such curly hair

6

Wishy washy, my name's Joyce She will have a smashing voice
Wishy washy, my name's Pip She will love to dance and skip
Wishy washy, my name's Joanna She will learn to play piano

Just as the last fairy was about to make a wish, the doors burst open and a huge voice roared:

What a jolly
party tea
Shame you haven't
INVITED ME!

It was the
Hairy Scary Fairy!

The Hairy Scary Fairy bent over
the Princess and pointed a long,
black wand.

The Hairy Scary Fairy told the King and Queen that their daughter would get stuck on a computer game for 100 years.

She wouldn't be able to stop until somebody could beat her.

Then the Hairy Scary Fairy
grabbed a cucumber sandwich
and ran out of the palace.

The King and
Queen cried and cried.
But even the Good Fairies
could not break the spell.

So the clever King ordered
every computer to be
thrown away.

The Princess grew into
a beautiful girl with curly
hair and a lovely figure.

She could sing and dance and play
the piano and everyone loved her.

One day, the King and
Queen went out for the day.
The beautiful Princess
stayed at home.

She began to explore the palace.
She found a tower she had
never seen.
As she went up the stairs,
she heard a funny noise . . .

BLEEP!
BLEEP!
BLEEP!

The noise came from a tiny room at the top of the tower. The Princess opened the door and saw an ugly fairy sitting at a computer.

BLEEP!

BLEEP!

BLEEP!

When the King and Queen came
home they heard a funny noise . . .

BLEEP! BLEEP! BLEEP!

It was the sound of Bleeping Beauty!
Bleeping Beauty played all day
and all night.

The King and Queen tried
everything, but they could
not get the Princess off
her computer.

The Princess was so good that
no one could beat her.
She never danced or played
the piano or even read a book.

I've only been
playing for
twenty minutes

No dear, it's been
twenty years

The King and
Queen grew very
old and still the
Princess would not stop.

A hundred years went by. The castle gardens grew like a jungle.

One day, a handsome Prince was passing by. He was the World Computer Game Champion. He pushed through the brambles until he found a huge door.

From inside he heard a funny noise . . .

BLEEP!
  BLEEP!
    BLEEP!

The Prince opened the door.
Everything was covered
in cobwebs, including the
King and Queen.

BLEEP!

The noise got
louder and louder . . .

B<small>LEEP</small>!

B<small>LEEP</small>!

The Prince crept inside.
He plugged in his console
and began to play.

Bleeping Beauty was good but the Prince was better. Before long he had won the game.

This game is boring anyway

said the Princess. She stood up and yawned and the spell was broken.

Suddenly the last
Good Fairy arrived.

Sorry I'm late

She waved
her wand and
made a wish.

Wishy washy,
my name's Nancy
She's the one the
prince will fancy

So the Prince and the Princess got married. They spent all their time reading lovely books.

But every now and then,
they would play one tiny
computer game.

BLEEP!   BLEEP!
        BLEEP!

ENJOY ALL THESE SERIOUSLY SILLY STORIES!

All priced at £8.99

Orchard books are available from all good bookshops, or can be ordered direct from the publisher:
Orchard Books, PO BOX 29, Douglas IM99 1BQ
Credit card orders please telephone: 01624 836000 or fax: 01624 837033
or visit our website: www.orchardbooks.co.uk or e-mail: bookshop@enterprise.net for details.

To order please quote title, author and ISBN and your full name and address.
Cheques and postal orders should be made payable to 'Bookpost plc.'
Postage and packing is FREE within the UK (overseas customers should add £1.00 per book).

Prices and availability are subject to change.